PARTS OF A PLANT

A Look at Roots

Lindsey Lowe

KidHaven PUBLISHING

Published in 2020 by
KidHaven Publishing, an Imprint of
Greenhaven Publishing, LLC
353 3rd Avenue
Suite 255
New York, NY 10010

For Brown Bear Books Ltd:
Text and Editor: Lindsey Lowe
Children's Publisher: Anne O'Daly
Design Manager: Keith Davis
Picture Manager: Sophie Mortimer

Picture Credits
t=top, c=center, b=bottom, l=left, r=right
Interior: Alamy: blickwinkel 7t; iStock: 8, 9tl, 16, 17b, 18; Shutterstock: 5, 9br, 10, 19, 20, Africa Studio 21, Allisa 4, Nikolay Antonov 12, Uwe Bergwitz 11b, Inga Gedrovicha 17tr, Matt Gibson 15t, Mirko Graul 15b, Lucy 14, Mykola Mazuryk 7b, Christian Mueller 11tr, E. G. Pors 19t, Bogdan Wankowicz 6, Tokaew Worachat 13bl; US Department of Agriculture: William Wergin and Richard Sayre, colorized by Stephen Ausmus 13t.
All other photos and artwork, Brown Bear Books.

Brown Bear Books has made every attempt to contact the copyright holder.
If anyone has any information about omissions please contact licensing@brownbearbooks.co.uk

Cataloging-in-Publication Data

Names: Lowe, Lindsey.
Title: A look at roots / Lindsey Lowe.
Description: New York : KidHaven Publishing, 2020. | Series: Parts of a plant | Includes glossary and index.
Identifiers: ISBN 9781534533738 (pbk.) | ISBN 9781534533752 (library bound) | ISBN 9781534533745 (6 pack) | ISBN 9781534533769 (ebook)
Subjects: LCSH: Roots (Botany)--Juvenile literature. | Plant anatomy--Juvenile literature.
Classification: LCC QK644.L694 2020 | DDC 581.4'98--dc23

Manufactured in the United States of America

CPSIA Compliance Information: Batch #BW20KL
For further information contact Greenhaven Publishing LLC, New York, New York at 1-844-317-7404.

Contents

What Are Roots?

Roots are a plant's supply pipes. They carry water and minerals from the soil up into the plant.

Most roots grow down into the ground. Most roots grow in soil. The roots of water plants grow down through the water. A few plants have roots that hang in the air.

Plant Parts

Roots are usually brown or white. Other plant parts above the ground are often green. All the plant parts work together to keep the plant healthy and make it grow.

THAT'S AMAZING!

Roots come in all sizes. The duckweed plant floats on water. Its roots are thinner than the thinnest hair! The wild fig has the longest roots in the world. This is a tree that lives in very dry places. Its roots grow up to 380 feet (116 m) long so they can find water deep under the ground.

Anchors

Roots help to hold the plant in the ground, like a ship's anchor. They stop the plant from falling over or blowing away in the wind.

How Roots Grow

Roots grow from a single root. They have pointed ends to help them push through the soil.

A plant starts to grow from a seed. It sends a single root down into the ground. This is the primary root. It is the thickest root. The primary root quickly grows branches called secondary roots. The secondary roots grow branches of their own. The roots keep on growing throughout a plant's life.

Bean Seeds

These bean seeds have started to grow. They have grown a primary root and secondary roots.

Root Caps

A root is made from tiny cells. They are much too small to see. Roots grow by adding more cells to the end of the root. The end of the root has a tough tip called the root cap. It protects the root cell underneath.

THAT'S AMAZING!

A single rye grass plant was found to have grown 7,000 miles (11,000 km) of roots in one growing season. That's long enough to stretch from coast to coast across the United States and back again!

Kinds Of Roots

Roots come in lots of shapes and sizes. Each type of plant has its own kind of root.

Some plants have lots of tiny roots. They spread out in all directions. These roots are called fibrous roots. Other plants have one long root that is much bigger than all the others. It is called a tap root. It pulls water from deep in the ground. Many trees have tap roots.

Grass Roots

Grass has fibrous roots. The roots are thin and branch out from the stem. They spread out close to the surface of the ground. Plants with fibrous roots help to hold the soil together. They keep the soil from blowing away.

Carrots

Some tap roots are very tasty! A carrot is one big, thick tap root. Carrots grow in the ground, with the leaves and stems poking above the soil. The plant uses its tap root to store food made by its leaves.

THAT'S AMAZING!

It is hard to find water in the desert. Some desert plants have a very long tap root to get to water deep under the ground. The mesquite tree's tap root can grow 200 feet (60 m) long. That's the height of a 20-story building!

Special Roots

Some roots have special tasks. They hold a plant up, or help it to climb. Some roots live in the air.

Some roots grow out from the stem. They help hold the plant in the soil. These roots are called prop roots. Corn plants and some palm trees have prop roots.

Stem Supports

Prop roots give extra support to the plant. As the plant stem grows, new prop roots grow higher up the stem. Many tall, tropical palm trees grow long, thin prop roots.

THAT'S AMAZING!

Some plants use their roots to climb. Ivy can grow up trees and buildings. Ivy plants have tiny roots along their stems. These extra roots produce a sticky substance. It lets the plant cling to trees and walls.

Dangling Roots

In a rain forest, the air is hot and sticky. It contains lots of water. Some rain forest plants grow on other plants' branches. These plants are called epiphytes. The roots soak up water from the air.

Roots and Soil

Tiny creatures live in the soil. They make the soil healthy. They help roots to grow.

Soil is full of tiny life-forms that are too small to see. Earthworms also live in the soil. These creatures help to keep the soil, roots, and plants healthy.

Earthworms

Earthworms burrow. They break up dead plants. Burrowing loosens the soil, which lets more air and water get into it. The earthworms leave behind waste called castings. These are full of nutrients that provide food for new plants.

THAT'S AMAZING!

Many roots have tiny worms called nematodes sliding around them. There are more nematodes on Earth than any other kind of animal! Root-knot nematodes crawl into roots. They form swellings, or knots, in the roots. These can kill the plant.

Good Bacteria

Microorganisms called bacteria live in soil or roots. Many plants, particularly pea plants, have bacteria called rhizobia living inside their roots. Rhizobia give the plant chemicals, such as nitrogen, that it needs to live.

Roots and Animals

Many small animals eat plant roots. Other larger animals use roots to make their homes.

Roots are tasty food for many small animals. Gophers and squirrels dig roots from the soil. They have sharp claws for digging. They have sharp teeth for chewing through tough roots.

Root Burrows

Some animals, such as gophers, make their homes under trees. The underground homes are called burrows. The animals dig their way through the soil to make their burrow. Tree roots prop up the soil as the animal digs.

Root Voles

Voles are rodents like mice and rats. They love to eat roots. If gardeners or farmers see chewed roots on trees, the chances are a vole has been at work. Sometimes voles eat their way through the roots of a whole orchard! They can cause a lot of damage.

THAT'S AMAZING!

Many insects live in roots. Swarms of tiny springtails live in soil and feed on roots. They get their name because their strong tails help them spring 20 times their own length into the air. That is like a 6-foot (1.8 m) person leaping over a tall tower!

Roots and People

Roots are where a plant stores its food. That's why some roots make healthy food for people to eat.

Plants make food with their leaves using sunlight. The food is stored in the roots for the plant to use later. People dig root vegetables out of the ground to eat.

Turnips

People have grown turnips for hundreds of years. Turnips are tasty and good to eat. The part that we eat is the large, rounded tap root.

THAT'S AMAZING!

Not all vegetables that grow in the soil underground are root vegetables. Many of them are simply parts of the stem. They grow underground for protection. Potatoes, onions, and garlic are stems.

Sweet Potatoes

Sweet potatoes are roots, but they do not have a single tap root like carrots and turnips. Sweet potatoes are swollen fibrous roots. They grow in hot places, such as Africa and South America.

Roots and Medicine

People have been using roots to make medicines for thousands of years. But some roots are poisonous.

Water hemlock looks like a tasty root, but one bite is enough to kill you. Mandrake root is poisonous, too. It makes people very sick and gives them nightmares.

Healing Roots

The roots of ginseng have been used to make medicine for hundreds of years. Scientists study plant medicines to find out how they work. They hope they will be able to make medicines using chemicals from plants.

Human Ancestors

Our ancestors probably ate roots as medicines millions of years ago. They learned which roots were good for healing and which were poisonous. Today, chimps eat plant roots to make them feel better.

THAT'S AMAZING!

Traditional Chinese medicine uses roots to cure illnesses! Ginger is used to help settle an upset stomach. The roots are usually dried and chopped up. Then they are added to hot water to make tea.

Grow It!

Carrot seeds can be sown in late spring. You can buy seeds online. You can plant them in the ground or in containers.

Here's How

- Make sure the soil is well dug and free from stones and weeds. Smooth the surface of the soil. Mark out rows about 6 inches (15 cm) apart and ¼ inch (0.5 cm) deep.

- Mix the carrot seeds with a little dry sand and sprinkle evenly along the rows. Cover with soil, then give them a sprinkle of water.

- The young plants will appear in about 10 to 20 days. Keep weeding the soil and water the plants once a week.

- After two to four months, the carrots will be ready to pick. Wait until the carrots are at least ½ inch (1 cm) thick. You don't need to pick the whole crop all at once. Leave smaller ones in the ground for a bit longer until they have grown.

- To pick your carrots, lift each one out of the ground gently, holding the bottom of their green carrot tops.

Cook It!

Carrot Cake Muffins are easy to make and delicious for breakfast!

- ½ cup vegetable oil
- 2 eggs, beaten
- 1 cup shredded carrots
- ½ cup milk
- 1 cup brown sugar
- 1 ½ cups flour
- 1 tsp baking powder
- 1 tsp baking soda
- 1 tsp cinnamon
- ¼ tsp salt

Here's How

1. Preheat the oven to 400°F (200°C). In a bowl, mix the vegetable oil, beaten eggs, carrots, and milk.
2. In another bowl, whisk together the sugar, flour, baking powder, baking soda, cinnamon, and salt.
3. Gently stir the whisked sugar mixture into the wet mixture in the other bowl. About 15 or 16 stirs should be enough to combine all the ingredients.
4. Put 12 muffin cups in a muffin tin. Spoon the mixture into the muffin cups.
5. Bake for about 20 minutes, then remove from the oven. Leave to cool, and then eat!

WARNING

Most cooking involves chopping ingredients and heating them in some way. Be careful as you cook and make sure an adult kitchen assistant is around to help!

Glossary

aerial root A root that grows high in the air on trees and walls.

ancestors People who lived a long time ago.

fibrous roots Threadlike roots that spread out in all directions.

primary root A plant's thickest root and the first to grow.

prop roots A root that grows out from the side of a plant to prop (hold) it up.

root hair A thin, hairlike side root on a larger root.

root vegetable A vegetable that is actually the root of a plant, like a turnip.

secondary roots The thinner roots that grow off a plant's larger, primary root.

stem The long upright stick of a plant that holds the leaves and branches up.

tap root A large primary root that grows deep into the soil.

Further Resources

Books

Aloian, Molly. *What Are Bulbs and Roots?* New York: Crabtree Publishing, 2012.

Dickmann, Nancy. *Q & A About Plants* (Curious Nature). New York: Powerkids Press, 2017.

Messner, Kate. *Up in the Garden and Down in the Dirt.* San Francisco: Chronicle Books, 2017.

Stewart, Melissa. *A Seed Is the Start.* Washington, D.C.: National Geographic Children's Books, 2018.

Socha, Piotr and Wojciech Grajkowski. *Trees: A Rooted History.* New York: Abrams Books for Young Readers, 2019.

Websites

https://kids.kiddle.co/Root

http://www.childrenoftheearth.org/soil-facts-for-kids/soil-facts-for-kids-10.htm

Publisher's note to educators and parents: Our editors have carefully reviewed these websites to ensure that they are suitable for students. Many websites change frequently, however, and we cannot guarantee that a site's future contents will continue to meet our high standards of quality and educational value. Be advised that students should be closely supervised whenever they access the Internet.

Index